C000185883

A
CHESTNUT GROVE PUBLICATION
FOR
SURPRISE YOUR IMAGINATION

www.surpriseyourimagination.com/run-the-valley
www.surpriseyourimagination.com/contact

A Chestnut Grove edition first published in 2021

Illustrations and text copyright © Tim Nash 2021

Concept conceived and designed by Tim Nash

Front Cover Photography – Renè Müller ©
www.lumachrome.photography

Back Cover Photography – Logan Fisher ©
www.loganrfisher.com

Introduction

Mental health issues, especially depression are on the increase worldwide across society, most notably in children and especially teens.

This book is written from the perspective of a teenager and so provides a backdrop pertinent to his age and life **but** the story is universal and crosses all borders of age race and gender.

It is a narrative where the central premise of the protagonist could be anyone. Depression can evolve, but remains a common enemy no matter if you are young or old, black or white male or female. Although the central thread here focuses on depression, the story also touches on other areas such as eating disorders, bullying and abuse.

Within these pages my aim is twofold:
First, to you who may be struggling with depression, in whatever stage, I hope you will find solace in words that were written from a place not dissimilar to where you might be. I don't attempt to offer solutions or help because quite simply I am not a professional and honestly still trying to figure it out myself. But, my own experience has taught me that to hear testimonies of how others are going through similar can be a comfort and maybe even remind me I am not as isolated as I think I am. I wish the same for you.

Secondly, to you who are coping with or simply in contact with someone who struggles with depression! It can be an almost impossible place to be, trying to understand why the person you love before you simply isn't coping with life and all you want is to help but don't even know what to do as it seems your words of well intended encouragement fall on stony ground. To you, I thank you and encourage you to never give up on that person, as hard as that may be, and I hope reading this book will help you understand a little better what depression feels like.

So, this is not a book exclusively for any one demographic, it is intended to speak to as many as possible and my aim, my hope is that it will be a catalyst to help all of us tackle and better understand this terrible affliction.

Prologue

Darkness held him hostage as the monster sank its claws of deception lies and hopelessness into his very soul. Theo screwed his eyes up trying to break free of its clutches, but it was often in the breaking of the day when after another restless night he felt as though he was suffocating under the pressure in his chest. He opened his eyes as the weary first signs of morning light shone its beams of light through the cracks in the blinds illuminating his room.

He grasped back some breath as the alarm on his phone broke the silence.

Part One

'Gooooooooooooooooood Morning Chicago! Another covering of snow last night and we're not getting above freezing today but beautiful blue skies and great music to start your day so whatcha got to be unhappy 'bout! Here's the one and only Bob Marley to start your day, coming up to one minute past seven!'

Theo slipped deeper under the duvet. What right has anyone to be so cheerful at this time, or even any time of the day for that matter he mused. These morning DJs must be on a constant supply of Prozac or something to be like that.

'Don't worry about a thing 'Cause every little thing gonna be all right Singin': Don't worry about a thing' Cause every little thing gonna be all right!...'

Whack! A lone fist launched from under the duvet to silence the lyrics but instead sent the phone tumbling just out of reach to the ground where the music still played.

What does he know, Theo grumbled to himself. Another person with the ol "smile everything will be alright attitude" who knows nothing about real life.

As the song faded, an overly enthusiastic commercial launched on unsuspecting ears.

"Hey, you, why so blue! Don't ya know life is a blessing?"

"Uh, oh yeah but you know, it's tough right now cus…"

"Yeah I know, bills to pay, but gotta be grateful for what ya got, right!"

"Wish it was that easy".

"It is friend, it is! Just purchase and download the new Happy App. today. Discover the secret to truly being content and watch those clouds disappear".

"Uh, the Happy App. you say?"

"Yes friend, it'll change your life".

A moments pause in the conversation and sounds of birds chirping away filled the airwaves.

"Hey, good morning"

"Well, I must say that's a huge smile on your face".

"Thanks to you recommending the Happy App. I'm a new man. Life is wonderful. The sky is bluer, the trees are greener, and all is well. If only I had discovered this miracle App. before then my life would have been so much better!

Sounds of laughter faded into the disclaimer message before the next song blasted its way onto the playlist.

During all of this life changing information Theo had started to doze back to sleep but it was another voice that jolted him awake.

"Morning Sweetie! Time to get up. You don't wanna be late for school. Nice hot tea here to wake you up!"

As he poked his head above the covers, he saw the back of his Mom disappearing out of his room and managed a yawn.

"Uh, thanks Mom"

He looked at the steaming hot mug of tea on his nightstand. Mom! She was the greatest and would do anything for anyone, but why did she still insist on bringing him tea in bed every morning when he couldn't stand the stuff. Maybe, he pondered, he might need to actually tell her one day.

With another yawn, one foot arrived on the floor followed, after a reasonable delay by the second and then his butt slid slowly but surely to the edge of the bed.

Sleepily he showered, brushed his teeth and fixed his hair before dressing. Same usual routine. Day in, day out. He might only be seventeen, but already this life seemed monotonous. He packed his textbooks into his backpack and slipped on his parka.

Mom was there reading her bible at the kitchen table as usual and looked up with a beautiful smile.

"Hi sweetie. How are you this morning?"

Pursuing an itch on his left butt cheek, Theo murmured something that only a Mother can interpret.

"Good, pleased to hear it. Shall I make you breakfast?"

"Mom! I've told you before, I'm nots a little kid. I don't need you making me breakfast anymore".

"Not even your favourite? Scrambled eggs and French toast?"

Mom's eyes twinkled as she knew she had caught his attention, but Theo stood his ground.

"Mom!" He pleaded as though facing torture before he opened the porch door and took a step outside.

"Love you sweetie" Mom called as she returned to her reading. Then, by surprise she received a kiss on her cheek, and as she looked up Theo was once again on his way out. "Love you too Mom".

The DJ was right, despite the fresh snow overnight and the sub-zero temperatures, the combination of the morning sun against the piercing blue sky made for a beautiful backdrop for the walk to school and as he turned the corner another sensation lifted his spirits. Cinnamon. The unmistakable aroma of cinnamon muffin wafting through the air enticing him, if he ever needed to be enticed, to his favourite coffee shop.

This was the best start to the day and although always popular, was well worth the wait. He loved the hustle and bustle atmosphere and yet there was something calm about the ambience too, and the customer service was the best ever.

"Good Morning, Welcome to Blue Coffee, where your beverage is as unique as you! What can I get you today?"

OK, Theo thought to himself as the barista smiled at him, maybe the greeting is a little cheesy but who cares. Nonchalantly he made his order.

"Ugggh, yeah can I have a, tall, extra hot, half-caff, half sweet, half whole milk, extra shot, capp, with touch of vanilla syrup, no foam, half sprinkle chocolate, half cinnamon, stirred anti-clockwise!"

The barista smiled utterly unphased.

"Anything else?"

"Yeah, a cinnamon muffin"

"Hey handsome"

Theo looked up from his phone to the barista.

"Huh, watcha say?"

The sweet aroma of cinnamon was now superseded by the subtle perfume of a beautiful blue-eyed brunette placed a gentle kiss on his cheek.

"Buy a gal a latte?"

It was one of the many things he loved about her, the simplicity of her drink order reflected how uncomplicated she was and for a moment he just stood in awe at this beauty before him and wondered again, as he had countless times before, why this high school ex-cheerleader had ever wanted to date him when she could have any jock around.

As they left Blue Coffee, the heat of their drinks warmed them against the bitter cold wind and Amy looped her arm around Theo as thy walked to school. After a short while, her grip became tighter.

"So, how was thanksgiving?"

He took a sip of his drink.

"Uh, it was, it was, well you know!"

"Can't Imagine how hard it must have been. It's a big milestone."

Theo nodded and the two figures trudged on through the snow in silence and yet somehow, he knew that she understood and had his back.

He thought of how strange it had been, carrying on with the usual traditions, helping Mom make the cranberry sauce, laying the dinner table with Faith, his kid Sister, and then watching the game. Yeah, the game! What a match it had been and a great victory for the Bears. So cool. And yet there was this gaping hole nagging away throughout the day. As a family they had tried to laugh, tried to say grace with genuine hearts and tried to keep the home warm with love from morning to night.

Without Dad the holiday would never be the same and they all knew it. Thanksgiving had marked a year since the fatal crash, but it felt as though time had frozen like the ground beneath his feet, and yet life all around went on as if nothing had happened. Sometimes he felt like just stopping in the middle of it all and screaming at the top of his lungs, "What's wrong with you all? Why are you laughing and smiling? Why are you carrying on as if all is well? Don't you get it? Don't you, don't you know he's gone!"

As if she could hear his thoughts, Amy stopped and pulling off her left glove gently placed the palm of her hand on his coat over his heart.

"He's here, Baby. He's always here."

As they walked onto the school grounds there was the usual nudging and whispering among some of the students as they watched Theo and Amy. They had been dating now since last Christmas Eve when Amy had made the bold move to ask him out for a coffee and once news broke after New Year, the rumours and speculation had begun. Nobody could figure it out. Why was this beautiful smart girl hanging out with what most considered to be a loner and a bit of a loser. True he was a good football player but he was never going to set the world on fire, and neither was he an "A" student and yet here they were almost a year on still together.

Amy had dated a couple of guys from the school team, but they wore their arrogance like a badge of honour and treated her like a trophy. Theo on the other hand had always been nice to her and it was the day when he raced to her side to help when she had truly seen him for who he was.

It was silly really. Amy and the other members of her cheerleading troupe were trying a human pyramid routine that would form part of the intermission entertainment during the next game but as she was launched into the air by two of her team mates their jealousy of her prompted them to spring her too high. She crashed into the girl on top and tumbled onto the ground hurting her shoulder to such an extent that she was injured for the rest of the season. As the girls laughed and pointed at her in mockery, Theo broke away from his training and ran over to her.

It was just instinct really but as he reached her and heard the mocking laughter, he was reminded of his own experiences of being bullied when he was younger. He reached out to her and lifting her into his arms carried her to the Nurses station. Neither said a word to the other but Amy's heart was melting at his gentle kindness and protective arms.

A dislocated shoulder meant that Amy was bedridden for the next few weeks, but Theo visited almost every day, bringing her schoolwork and even the occasional latte. Despite the pain he was carrying at losing his Pops he was so kind and made her laugh. His self-effacing nature made her fall for him, not that he seemed to know or even return the feeling. She dropped so many loaded hints trying to get him to ask her out but all to no avail so then she had taken matters into her own hands and asked him on a date.

That Christmas Eve was magical and although she knew he struggled with confidence and lack of self-esteem it only drew her closer to him. After all, it's not like she wasn't fighting her own inner battles.

Part Two

First up today was history, a class Theo enjoyed especially as they were studying the Civil War from a homestead point of view. He and Amy took their seats beside the window as Mr Severide raised his hand for all chit chat to cease and began the lesson.

For the first ten minutes Theo was fully engaged and made copious notes but then his mind suddenly shifted gear. He found himself zoning away from his teacher's voice and drifted very quickly into himself as he gazed out of the window to the football grid, track and beyond.

There was no apparent cause, no reason but tears unexpectedly welled in his eyes and he felt overcome with heaviness and despair. He felt isolated, lost and alone and then there was the tightness in his stomach that hurt considerably. For a moment he caught himself in the middle of this and physically shook his head as if that would dislodge the overwhelming sadness consuming him.

He blinked hard and deliberately tried to return his mind to the moment but instead felt worse. A little pep talk to himself, reminding him that it's ok to not be ok and that this will pass didn't help. It felt like his eyes were bulging out of his head and all concentration disappeared as he fell into some kind of weird out of body experience.

Then under the desk he felt a hand squeeze his and he turned to see Amy smiling sympathetically. She knew. She understood these moments and saw the signs. She also knew the best thing to do here and now was to reassure Theo and that physical contact was important. He returned the smile, but it felt fake, and he worried that she would see him for who he really was and walk away in a blink of an eye. His heartbeat felt elevated, and energy seemed to be disappearing fast from his body. He tried the breathing exercises his counsellor had taught him and although he remained in a state of upset, he at least felt like he could breathe again.

Theo had no recollection of the remainder of the lesson and really only made it out to the school cafeteria with Amy leading him.

"Why are you with me?"

It wasn't self-pity that drove him to ask the question but a genuine struggle to understand why anyone, out of choice would want to hang around him. He felt a failure and somehow thought his depression would one day overwhelm him to a point he would never climb back. These bouts of emotional loss had heightened since losing Dad but if he was honest, he had always struggled with confidence issues.

"Because you make me happy. You take care of me and you let me be myself!"

Theo shook his head.

"You could be with anyone you wanted!"

"Hmmm, true" Amy replied playfully looking around at the guys in the hall, before her eyes once again met his.

"And I choose to be with you. Better get used to it mister! Cuz, I'm not going anywhere! C'mon, let's get outta here and find a little fresh air."

They walked, talked and held hands tightly.

"Wish I didn't feel like this. I don't want to, really I don't. It's just like it hits me for no reason."

Amy nodded as Theo continued.

"I'm so grateful for all I have. I love Mom and Faith, and you are awesome. I thank God every morning, so why do I get like this. It's so confusing!"

"You've been through so much Theo! You really have. I'm amazed you get out of bed at all each morning."

"I don't dwell on my problems! Honest!"

"No, you don't. I know that, and I see you fighting every day. All I'm saying is not to give yourself such a hard time."

She drew him closer and kissed him just as the bell sounded for school to begin again.

Part Three

'Have you ever wanted to hurt yourself?"

The question was as stark as it was shocking. Theo spent most of his sessions with his counsellor staring either at the floor or at the picture of the mountains on the wall just over her shoulder but this question, or rather the answer he gave needed eye contact. With tears Theo looked up at Charlotte and slowly but deliberately shook his head.

'No." He said softly but firmly.

Charlotte's expression didn't really change and yet he sensed a warm smile. She'd make a great poker player he thought to himself as he pondered how she never really reacted to anything he told her.

This was a safe place, somewhere he felt he could truly be himself and be honest. Although the reality was he often felt drained after these weekly sessions because it felt like some kind of open emotional heart surgery was going on. Sometimes he clammed up, with nothing to say or just too overwhelmed while other sessions were filled with tears and pain. Theo didn't always feel he was making progress and told Charlotte he sometimes felt he was a fraud and wasting her time. A seasoned counsellor, Charlotte would reassure him and continued to listen to no matter what was said in their time together. She was skilled in asking the right question at the right time and listened intently to his ramblings as if he was the only one who mattered.

'How are things?."

'Nice guys finish last" Theo murmured.

Charlotte remained quiet and yet willed him gently to continue.

'Those mountains!" He said losing himself once again in the painting on the wall. "Where are they?"

"Oh, they are in Colorado I believe. You like the picture?"

Theo nodded.

"Is it deliberately there?"

"Deliberately?"

"Yeah, like a metaphor or something. I mean you have tons of students who come here and sit in this seat, right. And each one sees the picture."

"Why do you like it?"

For a few moments there was silence in the room, but as usual this was the one environment when silence wasn't awkward, and Theo was able to unpack some of the clutter in his head.

"Fresh air," He began. "It makes me think of fresh mountain air. Clean air. Open space where you can breathe and escape. Those peaks... yeah man, those peaks stretch up to the pure blue sky. Kinda like they are free too... but with a strong solid foundation of rock and," He paused, "And I like the snow on the mountains. Kinda gives it a sora cool feel."

Theo was lost for a moment in the peace of the picture.

"Just noticed" He said straining his eyes, "There's a bird, an eagle I think, flying over one of the peaks. He's, he's..."

Another pleasant silence before Charlotte gently encouraged.

"He's what Theo?"

"Free!"

"You said it made you think of escape?"

Feeling like a naughty schoolboy being caught out, Theo shuffled in his chair and removed his eyes from the painting back to the carpeted floor and remained silent.

"Do you ever feel like escaping?"

Tears were being choked back now as he grasped for air and the strength to reply.

"Yeah." He nodded. "Yeah, sometimes I just wanna run away from it all."

Part Four

It was a more positive Theo who appeared for football practice after school that afternoon and as he huddled with his team mates to listen to the coach, he gave himself a little encouragement.

"It's OK Theo. You are OK. give yourself some slack. Don't beat yourself up."

Truth was he still felt fragile, and it was the seeming randomness of how thew depression caught him out that affected him most.

"Gentlemen!" Coach Murphy's booming voice cut through the air. "The big game is coming up and I expect each and every one of you to be laser focused. We work as a team leaving no man behind but if you can't cut it then I'll have no hesitation in cutting you!"

He glared at a tall boy to Theo's's left.

"Fletcher!"

"Yes Coach!"

"Your performance against the Rams was subpar. I won't accept that kind of slackness again. Man up princess and do your job or someone else will. Understood!"

Fletcher straightened up and just short of saluting, barked his acknowledgment.

Coach was the typical bulldog leader, someone for whom defeat was a dirty word and who took such attitude as something personal. He knew what was said of him behind his back but neither cared nor tried to change because after all, he argued, the results on the field were proof of his tactics working. Not one of the players hadn't fallen foul of Coach Murphy, even when they had done exactly what was asked of them, and truth be known being chewed out by him was somewhat of a badge of honour. They all knew the fearsome reputation the team had in the league and that was almost entirely due to their leader. Of course, he would say it was completely down to him.

Theo completely disliked Coach but he loved the game and could fuel a lot of his energy out there on the field. He wasn't the greatest and nor would he ever be, but actually in those rare moments when he allowed himself the luxury, he felt that he was quite useful.

....

His first tussle with Coach had come early in the previous season when quite simply he had shown up five minutes late for practice due to his counselling session running over. When he tried to explain the reason, the exchange was ugly.

"Smith! Who do you think you are coming onto my field thirty minutes late?"

"Uh, sorry Coach but it's only five minutes and I..."

"You worthless piece of dirt. How dare you challenge me!"

"Sorry Coach but I..."

"You what? What brilliant excuse are you gonna give for letting your team mates down?"

There was an awkward silence as his teammates were now all watching and waiting like viewing some macabre show where the lion was about to rip its prey limb from limb.

"My counselling session ran over and I..."

"Counselling?" The roar and distain in that one word was culpable. "You're telling me you were late to the field of battle, where warriors fight and spill blood because you... you were talking about your "feelings".

Theo felt his whole demeanour shrinking as he feebly nodded.

"Well lads," Coach boomed addressing Theo's teammates, "Mr Smith here has just gifted you all with a reward for his tardiness. Now, all of you, ten times around the field, full sprint!"

With groans and looks that could kill aimed at Theo, the team started off and as Theo began to follow his shoulder was caught by Coach who growled at him.

"Listen up Smith. There's no place for feelings here. You're a great player. You've got potential but I'm telling you now real men deal with it out there on the field. So, whatever is going on in that pea sized head of yours, just snap out of it!"

It was ignorant. Thoroughly archaic. A mindless comment devoid of any understanding of the facts but four words that would actually have the exact opposite effect of any possible good intent they may have.

Somehow Theo had made it through that training session as his teammates, all one-time recipients in one way or another of Coaches bullying did their best to assure him of no animosity but he had walked home numb, playing the incident over and over in his head. "Snap out of it" rang like a dreadful anthem in his mind. He wrestled with how often he had said those exact same words to himself and how over the course of the last eight months his counsellor had helped him begin to let go of such self-assassination. Now, here he was again raising the gun and pulling the verbal trigger.

That night had been the first time he had sobbed, feeling as lost isolated and alone as he never had before. Sure, there had been tears before, but these seemed to come from his very soul. Of course, he told nobody. Not even his counsellor because he neither wanted the wrath of Coach Murphy nor the ramification of being benched from the game he loved which he was sure would happen. Besides, the team were second in the eague and on point to win the championship for the fourth year running, so there was no way the school would risk losing Coach. He could hear it now, "His bark is worse than his bite!" or "Oh that's just his way to motivate you". Scholarships were awarded due to how successful the team was and it was only ever going to be his word against Coaches.

....

That evening's training went as well as could be expected but focus was now most definitely on the upcoming big game and Theo for one felt the pressure and stress already welling up in his stomach. This wasn't helped by Coach pulling him to one side after the session.

"Not the worst performance I've seen from you Smith."

Theo waited for the touchdown which sure enough came fast.

"Look kid, I know you have these, these uh well troubles in your life. Hey, listen, who doesn't but I want you to take some advice from me, OK. Before you enter the locker room for practice or more importantly for the game, I want you to imagine a coat rack just outside. Then I want you to hang all your troubles and worries or whatever crazy stuff might be in your head on that coat rack. That kinda stuff doesn't belong here and I don't wanna see or hear it. You can just pick it up on your way out and take it home with you. Got it!"

It was cold and hard and an utterly ignorant statement.

As he watched Coach turn and walk away, Theo wanted to believe he was trying to earnestly give some valid advice but instead he felt hurt and wounded. As far as he could recall, he had never and would never bring his feelings onto the field. True sometimes he might be fighting inner turmoil, but he tried. He always tried.

Walking home that evening Theo felt despair turn to frustration, inner turmoil and then anger. He was angry at Coach. Angry at the World.

Angry at God. Angry at Dad leaving him. Most of all though he was angry at himself. He felt like such a failure.

Why did it feel that no matter how hard he tried to rise above depression he still felt oppressed down and in pain? He tried to be a good decent and honest person, a good son and Brother as well as a good boyfriend and bro to his mates. In his better moments, he knew he had a kind heart and always took time to listen to those around him when they needed support. And yet somehow he felt like life just kept beating him down for trying to do the right thing but even that didn't deter him from wanting to be the best he could be to those he loved. But if he was honest he felt like perhaps people sometimes took advantage of that, or maybe truth was he allowed them to. Yeah, he was angry at himself for sometimes giving away more of himself than he should.

The irony was that he really didn't want to change that part of him because it felt like it was the one truly genuine thing he could offer, and yet here was that self-loathing creeping in again for not being able to stand up for himself. Sometimes he knew the best way he could help those around him would be to take time out for himself, to recharge and then come back stronger. But if he ever did that, and it was very rare, then he just beat himself up for feeling selfish. Now here he was burning out and crashing to the ground like the saddest falling star ever. It was this confusion and lack of self-esteem that contributed to the anger inside.

His body tensed up and stress engulfed him. For a moment he felt like he might genuinely be about to break down.

Part Five

"God doesn't care."

The congregation shuffled uneasily in their seats.

Pastor Lee paused and looked out onto the sea of faces staring back at him. These were his flock, his family, his responsibility, and that weight played heavy on his heart and mind.

Two rows from the front Theo sat as he always did Sunday by Sunday next to Mom and Faith but in recent times he had felt less enthused with church and actually found that his own faith was taking somewhat of a hit. He had questions about a God who seemed to allow injustice to flourish in this world and quite frankly he felt like he had been let down after so many scriptural promises had gone awry. He questioned why God seemed to allow him to struggle with depression and felt guilty too for not being able to break free and live a life of joy.

Now though, it sounded like Pastor Lee was coming around to his way of thinking and Theo found himself on the edge of his seat waiting for the punchline, and what would surely now be truth preached for once.

"Family. God doesn't care." Pastor Lee repeated slowly and with a very determined tone. "He doesn't care if you are black or white! He doesn't care if you are young or old..."

"Ah!" Theo slumped back in his chair! "What a sell out!" he whispered under his breath as the sermon continued.

"Our text today, Psalm Twenty-Three, verse four..."

After daydreaming his way through the sermon, Theo came back to reality as the final moments of worship lifted his spirits, partly because Amy was part of the gospel choir and also due to the way the band rocked. With the service drawing to a close, the congregation drifted out of the auditorium and while some went about their daily business, others including Theo hung around for coffee in the church café.

He sat at a table playing on his phone as Mom and Faith went to get drinks and a snack but was momentarily interrupted with a slap on the back.

"Thought that was you! How are you Bro? You've been AWOL."

Theo looked up at the man's warm smile.

"Hey Billy, Yeah, you know it's been crazy busy recently. Football practice and stuff."

Billy nodded.

"Mmmm, I heard Coach has been driving you all extra hard. But you know it's important to take time out as well and we miss you on Fridays. Man! We miss you period. Justin was saying he hasn't seen much of you recently either."

"Yeah, I know." Theo waved his phone. "I'll message him."

"Good, good, yeah y'know a message would be cool but maybe give him a call too. He's your best friend and you may not realise this, but he needs you. Great preach this morning don't ya think?"

Theo shrugged his shoulders.

"Sell out." He murmured as his eyes caught Billy's.

"You didn't like it?"

"It was, it was fine!"

"So, you didn't agree with it?"

Theo shifted in his chair. He really didn't want to be having this conversation.

"Go ahead," Billy prompted. "Tell me what you thought."

All at once Theo was conscious of his own anger and frustrations and didn't want to show disrespect to the man before him, his youth pastor who was also Pastor Lee's son, and yet he had to say something.

"It's bs."

Billy continued to smile waiting for what was to follow.

"I mean God is pretty screwed up isn't he. He allows pain and hurt in this world even though his word says he won't allow harm to come to us and then he says he won't give us more than we can take and yet think about Bobby Jean last year. She didn't deserve that and yet it happened to her and then, and then she ended it all. Where was God then? She couldn't take it. He abandoned her just when she needed him the most."

Theo paused for a moment and as he spotted Mom and Faith chatting with some friends, then tears filled his eyes.

"It doesn't make any sense. Good people suffer. The best most loving kind and caring people are made to hurt. Why is that?"

Billy followed Theo's gaze to his family, and as his attention rested back on Theo he was very aware of all that had happened to them in the last year.

"Mom still cries. No, she sobs in pain. And Faith forgets sometimes and asks when Pops is coming home. It's not fair."

"No, no it's not fair." Billy agreed.

"Then," Theo now found himself growing in anger but could hardly get the words out, "then, then that man walks away without a scratch."

"'mon, where's the justice. God gives him a pass and yet he, he..."

"He what?" Billy asked already expecting the answer.

"He steals my Dad from Mom and Faith. A good hard-working man! God is not good or great. He's cruel."

In all honesty Billy felt out of his depth. In all honesty he had the same questions Theo did. It didn't make sense. A drunk driver had slammed into Theo's Dad's car with such force it pushed him off the road and into the Chicago river. There had been talk that he might have survived the initial impact, but the sub-zero temperature of the icy waters didn't give him a chance. Then to add even more pain to this incredible loss, the drunk driver had walked away without a scratch and had never to this day showed any kind of remorse.

"And what about you?" Billy asked quietly.

"Huh?"

"You said God had stolen him from your Mom and Sister! But what about you? You've lost him too!"

"Ah, who cares about me!"

Billy knew he could list a whole bunch of people who more than cared about him, but he was also wise enough to know that wasn't what he wanted to hear. Trouble was, he didn't know what he could say.

"It's OK to be mad at God! He can take it."

"Yeah, well maybe he can. But look at Mom, this has broken her. She can't take it. Listen, I know God has a plan and all of that stuff. I even know on my better days that God didn't cause the crash!"

Theo stood up before he continued.

"But he didn't prevent it either!"

....

There was a notable silence driving away from church before Mom spoke.

"I saw you chatting to Pastor Billy!"

Theo just stared out of the window, watching the wintry streets pass by.

Sensing she wasn't going to get a response; she tried another topic.

"I spoke to Mary today, Justin's Mom. Did you know he had been mugged?"

Immediately pulling himself up from the slump in the passenger seat Theo locked his gaze on her.

"What?"

"Mmmm, last Wednesday apparently. He had gone into the city and was jumped on. He's OK. Sounds like his pride took a beating more than he did."

Last Wednesday? Theo cast his mind back. Oh yeah Justin had asked him to go bowling, but that was a bad day for Theo as he had been struggling with stuff. Guilt washed over him like a tsunami. He should have been here. He could have done something. Stopped it.

Mom glanced over at her son.

"It's OK baby. He's OK."

The passing streets seemed to now bear down on him, to implode and suffocate him as feelings of failing his best pal consumed him along with one other thought. "Way to go God!" His thoughts were interrupted by the ever-sensible rational voice of his Mom.

"You can't change what's happened, but you can do something now. Get in touch. Go and see him!"

Theo was already typing away on his phone.

....

"You idiot!"

Theo grinned at his pal.

"What are you, getting beaten up by girl scouts!"

Justin laughed.

"Yeah but man! You should have seen them. Even the Rock would have run a mile. And boy were they u-g-ly! I mean not as ugly as your sorry face, but you know, getting there."

The two friends laughed but as Theo looked at his pals bruised face he still couldn't escape the feeling of remorse.

"I should've been there, man!"

"Oh yeah and what would you have done, scared them off with harsh language or maybe just breathed your nasty jalapeno breath on 'em! Nah, Man! It's cool."

"I'm sorry bro. Really am."

"Listen I'm telling ya, it's cool. We cool. To be honest This has done me a favour. Couple of days off school and you should see how my Facebook page is lighting up especially with comments from Michelle Laine."

"No I don't just mean this; I mean I've not been around much recently and... did you say Michelle Laine?"

Justin laughed again.

"Dude! She thinks I'm some kinda hero. She wants to hook up!"

"Bro! She's hot. That's like awesome."

Sitting back with his hands behind his head, Justin grinned rather pleased with himself then took a moment.

"Man. What you've been through. I mean I can't even... I don't know what to say. It's tough bro. It's too much. But hey listen up, I gots your back. You wanna go quiet on me, fine but know this, I aint giving up on you. We bad boys for life."

The two friends laughed.

"Now then," Justin continued. "You ready to have your ass whipped at Motal Kombat?"

Part Six

"Are you ever gonna be happy?"

It wasn't the first time he had asked the question of himself.

Theo stared at his reflection in the bathroom mirror as he pondered the answer. The longer he lingered on his own face looking back at him, the more acutely aware of his own self he became, but in some senses, it made him uncomfortable. He studied his own features and for a moment almost felt as if his own soul was now exposed.

"What's wrong with you? What-is-wrong-with-you?"

With no answer forthcoming from his own reflection, Theo finished brushing his teeth, took a deep breath and ventured out into the world.

His usual coffee and cinnamon muffin at Blue Coffee. His usual walk through the snow with Amy affectionally holding onto his arm. The familiar bell to call students into class. The same routine, the same people. Theo's heart felt heavy again this morning, but he really couldn't figure out why and he hated himself for it. Hanging out with Justin last night had been so cool and his mood had been lifted this morning as Amy regaled him with her review of the latest Netflix movie. Her laugh was so beautiful. Here he was counting his blessings, so grateful for having so much, so conscious that life was actually good, so why was that little black cloud still shadowing his mood.

"What's wrong with you?" He asked himself again.

Theo went through the usual timetable of classes. English, American History, Social studies and worst of all Math. 11th Grade had proven to be a tough one and it seemed they had barely even started. He hated math with a passion and especially this terms concentration on advanced algebra which just blew his mind and indeed he felt would have been the end of him had it not been for one very important detail, his math teacher, Miss Farmer. In all honesty, life at Lincoln Grove High wasn't actually that bad and aside from the bullishness of Coach Murphy, all of the academic staff were actually really cool.

"Yeah," he thought to himself as he sat with his friends that lunchtime, it wasn't either the staff or the curriculum, which was that bad, but the pressure from elsewhere that sometimes felt like a huge weight. The pressure of some, not all, of his peers. Lincoln Grove was a midway suburb of Chicago, not so overly affluent as some small towns but neither was it a rough place to live like others and as a result the high school was sought after which made it all at once culturally and socially diverse but also ramped up the academic and popularity stakes. Theo had a small but loyal group of friends, Amy, Justin Ben and Roxanne all of whom were down to earth honest and real about who they were and what life was about, and it was within this group that they would chat about the pressure to "be" in school.

Roxanne took a deep breath.

"Man am I sick of this!"

A straight A student with a pretty face short, cropped hair and thin appearance Roxanne was too real in her approach to life to be considered a geek and despised those who based success on appearance.

"She's a bitch!"

Her friends glanced at each other, each wondering who was going to field this, but it was Ben who had a secret crush on her who decided to brave the waters.

"Who?"

Taking a fierce bite from her sandwich, Roxanne looked up suddenly aware that she had spoken out loud.

"Ah! That stupid b-itch Shona Lewis."

Another glance among the friends but this time with a knowingness at the mention of the self-styled queen of Lincoln Grove High, a girl who would need to dive extremely deep to get into waters shallower than she was. The problem was she knew how to wrap others, mainly guys around her finger and with a flutter of her eyelids seemed to get anything she wanted which was perpetuated by her mega rich parents who lavished anything on their only child that she wanted.

Amy smiled and put her arm around Roxanne.

"What's happened?"

Roxanne took a breath and placed her cell on the table.

"Take a look!"

The attack was as cruel as it was calculating. Roxanne had decided to run for class president this year knowing that she would be up against Shona amongst others, but she felt strongly that her outlook and approach to life would bring a fresh and much needed perspective. She hadn't bargained for the dirty tricks campaign and plain outright name calling that would be a part of it. The social media posts held nothing back and went straight for the heart, bringing up issues that had no place or bearing in any circumstance let alone politics. Roxanne was smart and knew that there would be banter that might get a little heated, but this was nothing short of character assassination and a smear campaign.

Amy's eyes teared up as she read and then showed it to Theo Justin and Ben.

"We'll report her. The school has a '0' tolerance to bullying and that's what this is!"

Roxanne shook her head.

"What good will that do? The damage is done! Now the whole world knows. Nobody will vote for me."

Aside from the harsh name calling it was the last post that was the cruellest bringing to attention Roxanne's battle over the last few years with an eating disorder. Although she had never kept it a secret, neither had she considered it news to be broadcast but in a school of that size, it was impossible to always be totally private.

"You should still run!" Ben suggested.

"How can I?" Roxanne replied as her phone pinged a few times and more thumbs ups and likes came in on Shona's post, "Listen to that."

"You know it's not that they agree with her. Man! Most of them don't even like her but they just want to seem popular too..."

Ben was desperate to help but even he felt like his words were empty.

"Cmon girlfriend, let's go get you freshened up!" Amy stood up nodded at the guys as she left with Roxanne for the bathroom.

"What are we gonna do?" Justin asked.

Ben shook his head.

"Know what I'd like to do to Shona!"

"Yeah, right, like violence would solve anything. Besides you aint gonna!"

'Nah! Dude I didn't mean that! I meant sabotage her campaign! Why's life so tough man! I mean why is that sweet girl gettin' all this grief. This school rocks and sucks at the same time!"

The three all nodded in agreement.

From the pressure to wear the right clothes to the colour of your skin and from your accent to your physical appearance it seemed you were judged and put on show every minute of the day. From the jocks to the geeks and from the stoners to the so-called cool kids it felt like it was a jungle of self-acceptance and fitting in.

Part Seven

The monotony of life played its hand over the next few days permeated by the occasional pleasant moment of interest and Theo found himself mixing the ingredients of melancholia with optimism.

Finally, the school week gave way to the weekend and this Saturday was especially eventful as it was Faith's tenth birthday. Theo loved his Sister for the most part although he never understood her obsession with unicorns, but he most definitely approved of her taste in music, classic soul, something they shared.

Whilst her peers were crying over the latest boy bands, Faith would gently rock to sleep with her earphones playing Al Green, Aretha Franklin and Sam Cooke. To any outsider this would have seemed very strange, but the reason was simple, understandable and beautiful. Pops had been a huge fan of this genre and had even insisted on playing his songs to his unborn Daughter. For Mom, Theo and Faith, the memory of Pops settling down after a long hard day at the factory, kicking off his shoes and listening to a vinyl record was more precious than anything.

Over a special birthday breakfast of waffles and maple syrup, Faith gleefully and unashamedly ripped the gift wrap from her presents revealing a beautiful memories scrap book from Mom. The three of them sat huddled together looking at faded photos of Faith as a baby, Theo ducking under a jet of water from a burst fire hydrant and of course most precious of all, reminders of Pops. They laughed and pushed back one or two tears before Faith opened her other gifts and then leant back in her chair.

"I'm gonna throw up!" She pushed the plate of half-eaten waffles away from her.

Mom laughed.

"Too much excitement."

Faith nodded.

"Ok, maybe go and shower and calm down. You've got a big day ahead of you."

As Faith jumped down from the breakfast bar, Theo cleared his throat.

"Umm, don't you want my gift then?"

In a second Faith was back on her stool grinning from ear to ear.

"You got me a gift?"

"Yeah, and if you don't wipe that silly grin off your face, I just might not give it to you."

As her smile widened rather than lessened, Theo produced a huge box and placed it on the counter and Faith leapt at him, throwing her arms around him tightly.

"I loooooooove you Brother."

"You better wait and see what it is before you say that." He said winking at Mom. "It could be a slimy frog for all you know."

If there was an Olympic event for getting paper from a package, Faith would surely earn gold because before the wrap even had a chance to hit the floor she was already opening the box within and instantly let out the kind of squeal that only a ten-year-old girl can.

She pulled out the cutest soft unicorn in the world. Purple coat with a pink mane and a silver glittering horn. But that wasn't the best part because as Faith squeezed it, the unicorn spoke.

"I love you! You're my friend."

Faith squealed again and then somehow without letting go of her new best friend also managed to hug her Brother again before running to her room to introduce the unicorn to his new toy stable mates.

Mom smiled at her son.

"You're such a good Brother." She took a sip of her morning coffee. "Couldn't have been cheap!"

"Been saving up from doing chores around the neighbourhood! But that's nothing!"

"Oh?"

"Yeah, the worst of it is that when I went to buy it from Gimbels, just as I was taking it to the checkout, Coach Murphy was standing right behind me. So embarrassing. But it wasn't until I left that I realised he had a big floppy doll in his arms."

They both burst out laughing at the very thought.

....

That afternoon they arrived with Amy at Dave and Busters for Faith's birthday party. She had worn her very best jeans and unicorn t-shirt for the occasion although had protested harshly when Mom insisted Theo's present remained at home. Five of her best friends met her and after ice cream they sped off into the paradise of flashing lights and games dragging a rather tired Mom with them.

"She loves you; you know." Amy held Theo hand and kissed his cheek.

"I love seeing how you take care of Faith."

Theo took a sip of his soda.

"She needs me."

"You need her." Amy smiled.

"It's a year of firsts you know. I mean without Pops. First Thanksgiving, her first Birthday." He paused. "I overheard Mom crying last night. Wish I could make it better."

"You give so much baby, you really do. Another reason I love you, but you need to take care of yourself too."

"Nah! I gots to be strong. They need me."

He stopped mid sip.

"You love me?"

Amy shifted in her seat. She had heard it too. Three little words that she knew perfectly well in her heart but had never had the courage to say until they had now tumbled out so naturally.

"Yes, you idiot. You must know it by now. I love you mister."

Theo continued to look straight ahead not quite knowing what to do with this information but already his head was going into meltdown. Why? Why did she love him?. Actually no, maybe the question was how? How could she love someone who was so broken, such a mess? He felt like a failure and so undeserving of this. If she only knew how he struggled. If she knew of the conflict and turmoil inside, the self-doubt and even at times self-loathing. If she knew then she would run a mile. Actually he had been expecting her to dump him pretty much since the first date because let's face it, when it comes down to the wire," I'm screwed up."

Thoughts continued to ambush his mind.

'I'm so grateful for all I have. I get up every morning even though it's a battle and tell myself 'today is the day' I'll sort myself out. I'll be better and I'll conquer how inadequate I feel. But sometimes I just feel like the weight is too much. It's overwhelming. I don't want to be this way. I really don't. I try. I get up off the canvas every time to try again but it just feels like I get knocked down in no time at all and sometimes think maybe I should just stay down!'

He watched the people running around in front of him, playing games, laughing and having fun and couldn't imagine that any of them felt this way. It wasn't that he felt sorry for himself. Far from it. He deeply appreciated all that he had and knew that he was blessed, but it was just that sometimes he felt like he was suffocating and had little to no strength to fight back.

But then there were the contradictory thoughts. Glimmers of something else. Thoughts that were often suffocated by all else and yet called out like pin pricks of light illuminating the dark.

'I have my moments' he mused. 'I can be nice, and I can even be funny at times. I'm not the worst on the gridiron, despite what Coach says and I can even be a good son and brother at times.' Then there is this amazing girl sat beside me right now. As far as I'm concerned she's perfect. Beautiful smart, funny. She's loved by everyone and is a very talented artist. I mean, she chose to be with me. She accepts me and supports me. She's helped me through the roughest of times over the last year and has even talked about the future as if I'm a part of it. She's even been a listening ear to so many of my darkest thoughts.

He could hear the inner conflict. 'Yeah, but maybe she's just taking pity on you. It's not gonna last. She'll wise up soon enough.'

Why did he feel such a mess? Why did he seem to complicate everything? Why couldn't he just accept she loved him?

Theo came back to reality as he felt her soft lips on his.

"It's OK. You don't need to say it back. But I'm not going anywhere, OK!"

She took his hand and pulled him to his feet.

"Now then mister. Ready to be thrashed at Mario kart."

Part Eight

He had cried before but never like this. This was pure undiluted sobbing. Weeping as if from his very soul, a purging of something very deep inside as if there was a massive ache that was consuming his whole being desperate to escape via this river of tears. And yet within this attempt at freedom, to be released from such excruciating pain, Theo strangely felt nothing. It was like he was being held captive by some inner demon intent on his demise.

Before when the tears had flowed, it had been therapeutic, cathartic and although leaving him utterly drained would somehow serve a purpose, but this, this was having no such apparent end game.

He leant over and held his stomach which felt as if he had just been clobbered by the Hulk. Hah! The Hulk! Interesting that Bruce Banners alter ego sprang to mind because in this very room just a few weeks back he had related to Charlotte how he somehow identified with that creation of pulp fiction.

Theo felt just like Banner, always on the move always running. His head could never find rest and like the good doctor who was finding a way to contain and supress the monster within, Theo was constantly trying to defeat his own inner raging demon. Sometimes the pain and anguish of his depression made him feel like he was changing as Banner did into something that he could not control, and it felt when he had finally metamorphosized that just like the big green guy, communication to or from him became like an indecipherable alien language.

Wasn't there some song lyrics that said something about crying your heart out? In this moment Theo felt he could utterly relate to that but still there seemed no end to this uncontrollable bout of pain and as his face continued to be saturated with his tears he began to panic a little and felt his chest tighten.

Charlotte leant forward and calmly encouraged him to take some deep breaths.

"Focus on the mountains in the painting. Clean mountain air remember, wide open blue skies...breathe Theo, breathe."

Theo looked up at the painting and momentarily caught Charlottes eye. She was calm! How could she be calm right now as he was before her literally falling to pieces, and yet it was that very trust in her that all was actually ok which gave him pause to catch his breath for the first time in what felt like an age. He felt oxygen fill his lungs again, and that desperate suffocating feeling of claustrophobia began to slowly, ever so slowly lift.

Still clutching his stomach he leant back in the chair and weirdly felt the tears dry up rather abruptly. He shook his head as if coming out of some terrible nightmare and slowly scanned the room refocusing until he felt his heartbeat slowing and his stomach pain easing. He shook his head again but this time in confusion and bewilderment.

'What the heck had happened? Where had this meltdown come from?'

The reality was this had been one of his better days. He had gotten up in a pretty good mood all things considered. 'I mean nobody could call me king of the optimists,' he pondered, 'but as things go, this was a good positive day so far, so what the heck?'

He recalled walking across campus after the last lesson of the morning to come to this session and felt like he was making progress, even thinking maybe he could consider moving on from counselling. Yes, there had been a definite spring in his step.

He shook his head again.

Charlotte spoke.

'That was tough for you!"

He glanced fleetingly at her then at his sneakers then out of the window and gently nodded not knowing what to say.

That awkward and yet comforting silence filled the safe space of the room again and yet, despite looking out of the window, Theo could feel her eyes on him as she once again gave him space to be what and who he needed to be in that moment.

"Optimists!" He murmured.

"Optimists?" Charlotte repeated.

"They really freak me off."

Charlotte waited.

"You ever noticed something about optimists. They always ready to tell you that's what they are! They friggin announce it as if they superior or something. 'Oh look at me, I'm an optimist and the sun shines outta my backside!' Optimists! Why? Why do they hafta tell ya that's what they are, as if they're better than everyone else! Man, they kill me. It's like they wanna intimidate, or, or maybe it's just that in reality they the ones who insecure. Huh!, Yeah maybe that's it, maybe they hafta tell the world cus they don't want face up to their own failures or insecurities!"

Theo noticed a gentle nod from Charlotte but as she never voiced her opinion nor showed any kind of bias aside from total support of him, he wasn't sure if she had either given herself away for a moment by agreeing with him or if she was simply acknowledging him.

"I mean, I may not be the most optimistic person in the world, far far from it man! But I aint a fully signed up member of pessimistic anonymous either, you know! Nah man, I'm an optimistic with a heavy dose of reality in my pocket, but you know what, I don't need to shout it from the mountain. I aint no better than no one else but I aint no worse either…"

At these last five words, Theo stopped mid-sentence and somehow felt Charlottes eyes widen a little. Yes, he had heard himself too. "I aint no worse either'

This was the crux of it all. His own insecurities. His belief, almost religion that everyone else was better than him, that he was inferior and a waste of space. It was a tiring exhausting addiction to constantly be worried about what others thought of him and how they perceived him although part of his work with Charlotte had also led to the revelation that it was his own opinion and perception of himself that also held him in chains.

All the same it was fear of letting people down that sometimes landed him in trouble. Agreeing to something he really didn't want to do or not voicing his own feelings and opinions just for a quiet life and to please those around him. Of course such an approach isn't healthy and has a habit of coming undone. Eventually he would crack under the weight of promises made that he simply could not deliver and then he would either have to carry on to the bitter end or else bail and therefore let people down or hurt them because he couldn't cope. Either way it caused trouble and pain to others and proved all too often detrimental to his own health.

Guilt at letting people down or feeling inadequate would eat away at him as he unintentionally would dwell on his own perceived failures and this would feed his 'hulk' of depression. Sometimes he felt it was just impossible to live up to other's expectations of who they wanted him to be. Why couldn't they just let him be himself?

Theo often looked at others who seemingly could make decisions based solely on what they wanted to do and seemed to carry no remnants of second thoughts or guilt with them. Were they just hiding their true insecurities or was he just a messed up screwed up one of a kind who felt like little more than a slave to this behaviour even though he knew he deserved to be his own man and stand up for himself.

Once again he studied the patch of carpet before him, nervous to look at Charlotte.

"You've put in some really hard work here today, well done. I want to encourage you to remember you have a right to make your voice known, and it's ok if sometimes your words are not received. It takes time to rebuild what has been damaged, but you are making progress."

Theo left the session weary and tired. it was true that these sessions felt like an oasis in a world of chaos and now he had to live another seven days before the next one but despite it all, he remained determined. 'Even if, or more likely when I fall again' he thought to himself, 'I'll carry on."

Part Nine

They sat beside Lake Michigan on "their" bench, glad for the warmth of each other and of the hot chocolates they were enjoying. Although the wind was biting, the view of the frozen lake was spectacular and as snow began to fall once again Amy cuddled closer to Theo as they reminisced about their first date and how they had ended up walking along the lakeside before that first awkward kiss on this very seat.

One of the things he loved about her was this sort of unspoken language between them and that neither of them bothered with polite conversation just for the sake of it and yet they seemed to instinctively know what the other was thinking.

They began to walk back into the city.

Theo knew there was a great deal more to discover and understand about her because there were moments when the veneer of her apparently confident exterior would show the very slightest of cracks. In a world where you were bombarded constantly by adverts for beauty products, fancy clothes and where you couldn't turn on social media for so called influencers telling you to be this or that, Amy was a breath of fresh air. She was gorgeous. No question of that and if she so wanted she could probably coast along very nicely in this life on her looks and beauty alone, but that was not her style. Actually it almost seemed at times as though she felt this was a hindrance rather than a help.

"The world doesn't see me." She remarked. "They don't see or care about the real me."

It was true and it was the reason that Amy had pretty much withdrawn from social media in recent months due to the increase of comments that weren't just lewd but at times X-rated, but neither was she about to just disappear into the shadows.

Motivated by the online bullying and objectification she had begun a movement at school to empower other girls who felt the same but ironically this too bought her into another world of cristism as some accused her of activism or stirring up trouble. This simply motivated and empowered her even more and just this term she had been greatly encouraged to receive full backing of what she was doing from the school principal. With this and Theo's support she had quit the cheerleading team to focus on what she saw as immediate doorstep social justice.

Although he didn't feel completely able to say the words out loud, Theo loved her. Yes, he couldn't deny that he felt incredibly blessed to have such a beautiful girl in his life, of course looks played a part in that, but it was her heart which he had fallen for. There was definitely something about her, an aura and a spirit as well as that spark in her which actually moved him greatly. If he was honest, he was a little in awe of her. She was smart and had just last term come top of her class, but she was so much more than that, she was gentle and kind, giving and loving. Theo was still trying to figure himself out, who he was and certainly still really wasn't sure what he was going to do with his life, but Amy seemed, on the surface at least, to have it sorted. Inspired by Miss Farmer, she had decided to become a teacher although with an absolute distain for that particular subject she was focused on art.

As they arrived on the steps of the Art Institute of Chicago, Theo paused and pulled a few bucks from his pocket handing it to a homeless lady. All three exchanged words and Amy smiled at the kind heartedness of this man she loved before they went inside and found themselves looking at her favourite painting 'Nighthawks'.

"It's so melancholic." Amy whispered. "I mean I've sat here looking at it like a hundred times, but it always makes me sad. It makes me think of…"

For a second Theo thought her voice seemed to crack a little and he squeezed her hand.

It always happened here. This was the place where Theo knew there was pain inside her, something that troubled her and something that seemed to make her vulnerable.

"I'm scared."

Theo was taken back and stared at her.

"Why? Of what?"

She remained silent for what seemed an age as she closed her eyes.

"There's something... if you knew.... I just can't...."

Theo was worried.

"What baby, what is it?"

"I'm scared you'll leave me!"

His stomach tightened.

"I'm doing my best hon. I'm standing tall and I love you, but I'm scared you'll leave me if you knew the truth."

He touched her face and looked deep into her eyes.

"Leave you! Girl, you crazy! Why would I do something stupid like that? If anything I'm the one who should be scared you're gonna leave me! I mean, you smart and beautiful! Why would you stay with a loser like me..."?

"I'm broken." Amy's words interrupted his flow.

His eyes widened with questions and confusion.

"There's stuff I don't... I mean there's things i..."

Her eyes began to mist over.

"Babe, it's OK, you can talk to me. You can trust me."

Amy smiled. She knew that she could talk to him about almost anything. It was another part of him she adored, his broad shoulders weren't just physically strong but were always able to support her and others emotionally too. But could they take her secret, her shame? She was genuinely wracked with fear that her past may prove too much for him to bear.

She held him tightly, almost as if she feared this might be the last time. For so long she had worked hard to fight against the prejudices and objectification of others towards her, but he saw her for the woman she was inside, the one she really wanted to be known for. She exuded the best possible version of who she could be but in reality there was an insecurity within her, something she had long been afraid to face up to.

There was a strange silence between them on the train back home, neither quite knowing what to say to the other but as they walked from the station Amy loosened her hand from his grip.

"I got high!"

"What?"

"Last month at my last cheerleaders get together! Belinda asked me if I wanted something and i... well babe, I just needed to forget who I was for a moment, you understand don't you..."

Theo stopped and stared at her. He was confused.

"What? I, I... What? Forget what?"

He rubbed his face, trying to understand what she was saying. He certainly wasn't meaning to judge her, but this...this was shocking to say the least. It wasn't as if drugs were something that only happened in the movies and he had certainly been at enough parties to be offered everything and anything. He had even come close to taking on more than one occasion at the thought that he could escape his depression with popping one pill or another, but he had also seen lives of friends wrecked by this culture and somehow, by the grace of God had manged to always say no.

"I'm so sorry baby." Tears flooded Amy's eyes. "It was just one time. I hated it. I had nightmares for days after. I was sick. You remember I didn't come to school for two days..."

"Because you were recovering from using?"

Theo could hear the almost condemnation in his own words and he hated himself for it, but he felt hurt and betrayed.

What else was she not telling him. Then of course his own low self-esteem kicked in. Well of course what do you expect, you date the most beautiful girl on campus even though she's outta your league, so of course it's gonna end. You don't deserve her, you never did, and you certainly don't deserve to be happy, to have a life that's simple and good and easy. He could feel his inner demon of self-denial winning and blinding him to what really mattered in that moment; Amy!

Then the one thing he thought he would never struggle with and in that one moment we all have from time to time, in that heartbeat that will spawn regret for something we don't truly mean, he reacted.

"Are you crazy! I can't believe this. What were you thinking?"

His heart ached to see her broken and sobbing before him, but his blood was up and although all he wanted to do was hug her, he felt couldn't, almost as if he was pressing that self-destruct button again.

"I knew it. I knew you would hurt me one day. You hate me don't you. I mean why else would you do this to me."

"Baby, I'm sorry I didn't mean to hurt you. I, I was just..."

"What?" The purple haze of anger was taking over.

"I'm broken."

Theo shook his head.

"What the heck does that mean. You said that before. We all broken…"

"Baby"

"Nah!" Theo raised his hand, "Nah, I can't deal with this."

He was being a self-righteous grade A hypocrite and he knew it despite the angels of his better nature calling out to him he couldn't stop backing into the shadows of his own hell.

He turned his back on her and walked away even though every fibre of his being was telling him what a selfish s.o.b. he was. Maybe it was pride, maybe pain, maybe his own lack of self-esteem that told him he didn't deserve to be happy as he carried on walking and her sobbing faded into the distance. This time his self-destruct was taking her down with him.

Part Ten

'Great job Theo, great great job!' As he lay on his bed that evening he felt wracked with guilt and pondered how he had done it again, how he had taken something so good and wonderful in his life and then demolished it. The thing that amazed him most was how long it had taken him to ruin things between him and Amy. Amy! OMG! Amy! He curled up on the bed consumed by self-loathing and hatred for how he had treated her, someone that had been so amazing to him, someone who actually seemed to love him. He shook his head in disbelief of his own actions and the pain he had caused her.

What was it she had said, she wanted to 'forget'? He hadn't even given her a chance to explain and at the end of the day he knew her well enough that something must be very wrong.

....

'I hate myself. I'm just weak and pathetic'. Amy snuggled under the covers but couldn't find comfort and just kept replaying the conversation with Theo and how she felt she had let him down. She couldn't shake the look of disappointment and pain in his eyes and couldn't escape the guilt of how she who had caused that. Tears flowed down her cheeks as she remembered how Theo had first come to her rescue that day on the field and how she knew almost instantly he was someone special, someone who would be her best friend, and yes even someone she had dared to allow herself to love. That was hard all things considered, to expose herself and show vulnerability by saying those three little words but she meant it because in Theo she had found someone who accepted her for who she was beneath the skin, someone who made her feel safe and secure. Theo had often said to her that he felt it was a one-sided relationship, that he was the one receiving everything and yet the truth was that Amy felt she had found her soulmate. Now though she was convinced she had wrecked all that.

....

"Baby, are you OK?"

Theo fought back the tears that seemed trapped in his throat.

"Yeah Mom, I'm fine."

Although there was silence on the other side of his bedroom door, Theo knew she was still there. Knowing her she was probably praying or something and goodness knows he needed any help he could get.

Ping!

He picked up his phone and read the message from Amy.

'Babe kno I let u down. I'm sorry. Can we talk?

Theo's fingers lingered over the keys and then he typed

'Hey, I don't kno wot to say...'

Deleted.

'Wot happened? Why u....'

Deleted.

'Sorry I hurt u...'

Deleted.

Ping!

Another text from her.

'Kno I screwed up. Still love u. Forgive me.'

Theo closed his eyes tightly, fighting so much contradiction in his own mind. Why couldn't he just tell her it was ok, why couldn't he just reassure her. Man! When it came down to it he was the one who had messed up time and again and he was the one who needed forgiveness, but truth was there was a part of him who felt like he simply didn't deserve her and maybe this was just karma underlining the fact.

And yet he was terrified. So very afraid to let go, to wave goodbye to the best thing that had ever happened to him. Amy had always been there for him, even in those truly darkest of moments and even when it felt there was no damn good reason for his depression. His self-loathing seemed to whisper to him that he was and would always be a failure.

Ping!

....

Tears were soaking her sheets as she sobbed deep from her heart. Through the moisture of her eyes she kept staring at the screen of her phone, desperate to see a reply from Theo but still nothing. She felt like she might be hyperventilating and, in a moment to catch her breath flung the cover off just as her phone made that distinctive sound.

'Ping'

She retrieved the phone from beneath the duvet all at once excited and yet suddenly very full of dread for what the response might be. What if he hated her? What if he wanted nothing more to do with her? She needed him and couldn't bear the thought of a life without him but as she tightly gripped her phone she took a moment. If this was a rejection then she could postpone it just for now and pretend that they were still cool, that all those plans they had discussed for the future were still very much on the horizon. Her head was hurting so much, and she felt incredibly dizzy as she slowly turned the phone over to read the message.

Her heart sank.

It seemed these days that Theo's phone was full of pictures with Amy and himself and he scrolled through the gallery, zooming in occasionally on her face and that million-dollar smile as each photo evoked its own special moment and memory captured in time.

As he scrolled, he suddenly realised that just in those moments he had stopped crying and that the weight of that storm cloud hanging over him seemed less of an intimidation. His stomach was still knotted, and he still felt about as desperate as he could be, but the connection with Amy was something that helped take him out of his circumstances and more importantly displaced the depression if only for a short time, but nevertheless it was a welcome break.

As he scrolled through the gallery a headline popped into his feed and opening the link his heart missed a beat as he read of the breaking news that a young black man had been shot dead by a cop in Miami. Phone footage of the incident was lighting up social media clearly showing the man raising his hands before the deadly shots rang out.

Theo instinctively closed his eyes and prayed for mercy, but this story brought him back to reality with a thump. It was another reason he struggled in this life. He struggled that his own seemingly insignificant problems consumed him so much when there was true heartache and pain in the world like this. He constantly felt guilty for battling depression when he knew how blessed he was and how much he had to be thankful for, but it was hard not to be cynical. There was so much suffering in the world, poverty and inequality, starvation racial injustice and people trafficking, the list felt endless. These were the people who had a right to be depressed, they had a right to pain, not him, he was sitting pretty and yet, and yet as much as he knew that and believed it, as much as he counted his blessings he still found himself wrestling the beast of depression.

He could the voices of others. Voices that quite frankly didn't need to utter a word because he was already beating himself up with the same things.

"Be grateful for what you have. Man up. Get over it. There are others worse off than you. So many in this world would give their right arm to be where you are. Don't dwell on your problems..."

Yes, he had spoken every cliché in the book to himself, but the trouble was it simply wasn't that easy. Depression is not something that you can simply switch on and off like an Xbox. Depression is no respecter of rationality or common sense. It doesn't discriminate sex colour or creed. No, it's a deceitful subtle voice that lies and cheats its way into your head.

He also thought about those other voices. Ignorant and naïve that were simply not helpful but if anything could just add to the weight of self-assassination.

"Misery likes company. Don't sweat the small stuff. Make sure your glass is half full and not half empty. Smile, it will be ok. Just be happy."

He read the news article in full and felt his heart break again and the story developed revealing the man's kid Sister had been hit by a stray bullet. This is a cruel world, he thought to himself. It's a mess and makes no sense. Why God, why? He also took a moment to remember what was important, what truly mattered.

....

'Hey girl. How'd the date go? U tell him? L.'

Amy loved Roxanne. She was like a Sister and the two of them had a special bond and understanding that meant the world to her but bless her, at this moment it was not the message she was hoping for.

'Bout the party, yeah. Not the rest'

'U OK?'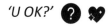

'Babe! Wot happened?'

"I've lost him. It's too much.' 😞

'No Amy. He's one of the good guys.'

'Don't deserve him.' 😞 😣

"Yeah u do. But girl u gotta tell him everything. U gotta fight for him. U strong, girl!' 😎

Amy paused. Her secret was almost too much to bear, and it had taken all the courage she could find to confide in Roxanne, but did she really have the strength to tell Theo? She knew and supported him for the counselling he was in but what would he say to hear she had been in therapy for the last two months too.

That alone was huge, but the reason for even going into counselling in the first place was something else altogether. She felt like a fraud and hated herself for not trusting him enough. She felt like a hypocrite too, encouraging him with his counselling and seeing a real need for him to pursue that course and yet doubting her own credentials for the same. After all maybe she had deserved what had happened to her. Truth be known it was being with Theo, seeing his courage at battling his depression that had encouraged her to seek help. She needed to be free of the past for herself but also because she wanted a future with him and knew she had to deal with the past to be free. The same old feelings of shame and guilt filled her head but now were joined by fear of telling the man she loved the reason why taking drugs that night was just a one-off desperate attempt to escape, to forget. She had been stupid and would never do something like that ever again. Apart from the comedown afterwards, she had immediately realised this wasn't going to solve her pain and knew right away that the fear of losing Theo was far greater than some stupid temporary way of numbing things. She knew she had needed to tell Theo and had intended to explain but a combination of nerves and fear meant she had tripped over her own words and somehow made things worse.

'I know. But he's ghosting me!'

'Give him time babe. He'll come around.'

'I hope so. It hurts so much.'

Part Eleven

It was the day of the big game. A rivalry full of passion and pageantry. Lincoln Grove Eagles would host the Washington Browns in a battle for supremacy. The Eagles had snatched victory in the dying seconds last season and if truth be told few that evening had thought a comeback was even possible but a last-minute touchdown by their star quarterback Mitch Andrews had stolen victory from the jaws of defeat. The last play of the game had in no small part included Theo whos' famed right arm throw had perfectly placed the ball into Mitches grasp for him to then storm over the endzone. Coach wasn't impressed despite the victory and had vowed to never again play the game that close to the edge so the last year had seen an even tougher regime than usual to the training, bordering on near obsessiveness.

Most of the players had their routines and their little superstitions that they went through with the belief this would help them secure that victory.

Although he wouldn't ever admit it, Greg Kidd would kiss his picture of Tom Brady seven times. Chaz Gibson had to go for an eleven-mile run and then drink a glass of raw eggs mixed with turmeric. Kelly 'the killer' Malone could only hit the field after cleaning his football helmet not once, not twice but five times.

Even Coach Murphy had a tradition, although his had a far deeper meaning as before the big game he would sit in the locker room before anyone else arrived and pour some whisky from a small silver hipflask into a paper cup and then hold it aloft.

"To you!"

He never drank the whisky. Actually he didn't touch alcohol ever because he had seen the effects it could have when his old man had been out on the town and would come back home 'punch drunk". 'Ha!' Murphy

58

thought to himself, what an ironic phrase considering that's exactly what would happen as his Dad would use him and his Mum as punching bags. He tried all his life to measure up to what his old man seemed to want from a son, but it was never enough. Never! And here he was today, a failed marriage and two estranged kids and still trying to prove himself to a man who was now banged up for life for killing a guy while driving under the influence last thanksgiving.

"Maybe today will be enough for you! Go Eagles"

Of course, none of this pre-game preparation mattered without true skills on the field and also a very real sense of camaraderie amongst the players. They trained hard together, trusted each other and had become a well-tuned fighting machine.

....

Theo didn't have anything in particular that he needed to do to prepare other than to focus and concentrate on the various plays and set pieces that had been drilled into them. Gameday was always stressful but today was not going at all well. He had hardly slept last night, tossing and turning battling depression and beating himself up over how he had treated Amy. He was still very confused as to why he felt so weak, so inadequate and so unable to send a simple text to her. He hated himself for it.

Physical fitness and mental confidence are key for every game and Theo knew today he especially needed to be focused so the combination of sleep deprivation depression and guilt seemed to suck all of that away. The pressure was immense, and he knew all eyes would be on him, from Coach to his teammates and from the Principal to the home crowd. Actually the game had received so much hype that even the local news station would be covering the evening just to add to the pressure.

He had slipped out from home early that morning to avoid Mom and Faith but as he sat in a far corner of Blue Coffee, he even felt guilty for that.

It was hard to focus or concentrate, not unheard of for Theo as his depression seemed to incapacitate him from these simple exercises at the best of times. He caught himself as so many times before just staring off into the distance, totally unaware of his surroundings and then would come to his senses not sure of how much time had passed. His usual favourite cinnamon muffin remained untouched.

The other customers laughed and carried about their day as if they hadn't a care in the world. Some were wearing Eagles jerseys and there was a palpable buzz and anticipation of this evenings game in the air.

It was too much. Theo went from being utterly oblivious of it all to suddenly deftly aware of every voice, every laugh and every person. He stood up abruptly pushing and stumbling his way outside into the bitter wind and snow, disappearing into the horizon.

....

"Hey! How's it going?"

As she picked up her phone Amy did her best to sound calm even though she was still hurting inside, but despite her façade Ben sensed something wasn't right.

"Uumm, yeah, you know. You, don't sound... right? You OK?"

"Nah, I just had a lousy night, you know."

Ben wasn't convinced but made a mental note to text Roxanne a s.o.s.

"Hey, you heard from TJ today"

Amy took a breath and stretched some of the tension out of her neck.

'Umm, no not heard from him since yesterday!"

'Oh! OK!" Ben was at a loss and Amy sensed it.

'What's up?"

'Hey, it's probably nothing but you know Justin and I usually hook up with him for coffee the day of the big game, but he was a no show and aint been replying to messages!"

Her heart sank. This was not like Theo at all. Despite the struggles he faced and the challenges he went through, he still maintained may great attributes, powering though difficult situations, always being there for others and always turning up on time where he was needed. The memories and pain of yesterday came flooding back in a new wave that knotted her tummy.

"I gotta go!"

Amy rushed downstairs pulling on her coat as she moved and virtually flew out of the front door with her phone to her ear calling Theo but with still no answer, she knew she had to find him.

Part Twelve

It wasn't the first time Theo had been at this spot in the city, but he really wasn't sure how he had gotten there other than some kind of inbuilt instinctive auto pilot but now he wasn't even sure why he was here. As forecasted, the cold weather had worsened and aside from the heavy snow falling, the biting wind screamed over the frozen Chicago river and seemed to slap him painfully in the face. If he could have found the tears then he thought they might actually freeze to his cheeks and as he gazed down at the icy surface and glanced around him he pondered on how meaningless life felt. A snow plough busied itself and the occasional fool hardy soul could be seen leaning into the blizzard, but it was the snow itself that Theo noticed more than ever. A white blanket covering everything, buildings, the road, the bridge, the railing and even topping the icy river. It was a cliché, but it really did seem like the snow was a metaphor for new beginnings, a veil of purity over the pain of the past.

He looked down at the river one more time.

"Miss you Pops. It's tough without you... you know... I mean I'm trying. I'm trying to be the man of the house, trying to be the best I can. Dunno... it just feels, I feel like... man I'm sorry I don't know what to do. It hurts Pops, it really hurts."

Theo's mind went back to playing touch football as a kid with his Pops in the back yard. His Pops had been his hero and he respected the man like no other. He knew he hated his job but loved his family and carried on day after day to ensure bills were paid and food was always on the table. He was a firm but fair Father who encouraged his children but never pushed them and lived a life very much by example. Theo felt he had been robbed. He felt life had dealt the cruellest of blows when Pops had been taken so suddenly. 'Yeah, life really is meaningless!'

And yet somehow, although he had been to the spot where his Pops car had gone over into the water a dozen times, this felt different. He felt a strange kind of strength as if he had permission to say goodbye to his Pops and stop holding on to that particular pain.

Some kind of peace filled his spirit and although he was still overwhelmed with depression he had courage within.

"I'll never forget you. Promise. Love ya Pops. I gots to let go. I gots to take better care of Mom and Faith, and…" He hesitated. "…and Amy! You'd like her. She's beautiful but she aint no fool. Just dunno how to fix it! Wish you could tell me what to do like you always did."

He raised a hand and waved goodbye.

....

Walking through the snow was hard work and it felt as though his direction was aimless but then he found himself by the lakeside sat on his and Amy's bench. This whole time he had been thinking of her, missing her and wanting just to hold her. He reached into his pocket and wrote the text he should have written long ago.

"I love you too. I'm sorry. Wish we were together right now." 🖤 🖤 🖤

He lay down on the bench feeling physical and emotional strength fade away from him.

As the wind continued to scream in his ears he thought it almost seemed to speak to him, distantly calling his name.

He blinked and shook his head. 'Oh great' he thought to himself, 'now on top of everything else I'm hearing voices!'

The cold was having a detrimental effect on Theo and he became strangely tired, almost as if he was going to pass out. A tugging at his scarf caused him to open his eyes and find a cute little dog pulling as if willing him to get up.

"Hey! Where you come from?"

"We are together!"

"Huh" What now, first the wind and now the dog was talking to him. He pulled himself to his feet straightened up and then felt soft lips on his cheek.

Amy!

"What, Amy-what you doing here? How you find me?"

Amy laughed.

"Oh yeah, like it was that hard to figure out. Babe you can be a lot of things, but a master of espionage aint one of them!"

"Baby, I'm so sorry. I'm so sorry for not supporting you, for not listening to you. I can't believe you came to find me!"

"Hey it's ok. We're ok, now come on let's get some hot chocolate and thaw out."

As they began to trudge back through the snow Theo suddenly remembered the dog.

"Where'd that little guy go? That little dog?"

"What dog?" Amy looked puzzled. "There's no other sane living being out in this weather"

"But there was this dog who kept me from passing out..."

Amy laughed.

"Babe, I think the cold has gone to your head."

"I swear. This dog it kinda like appeared, woke me up then disappeared!"

"Maybe it was an angel, a sign!" Amy laughed.

Theo rubbed his face and looked all around the lakefront, but it seemed to be true, they were alone. 'Maybe it was an angel' he thought to himself.

"Marty!!!" A distant voice caught it itself on the wind. A voice calling his Pops Name!

"Marty!!! Oh they you are you naughty thing, I've been looking everywhere for you. Don't you run off again!"

The figure picked up his dog and as they walked away, Theo smiled.

Part Thirteen

With hands wrapped around the steaming cups, their favourite hot chocolate slowly bought life back to their fingers and lifted spirits.

"You had me worried back there. Don't do that to me again or else you'll be in trouble mister, you hear?"

Theo nodded and texted Mom to let her know he was ok as Amy continued.

"Whatever happens in this life, whatever you're going through or feeling, you've got people who love you and care so much for you, and besides..."

She playfully grabbed him by the collar, "Don't you get that we need you too. You're always there for us, and it's you who pulls us together."

Theo gave a half-hearted nod and then looked at Amy.

"Hmm, don't know bout that. I mean look how I treated you. Sometimes I just can't get out of the funk I find myself in that I feel totally locked up and selfish."

"Babe, it's not easy for you. I mean this has been a tough year for you but even before then you were struggling with stuff. You're entitled to think about yourself sometimes but in all honesty I don't think you do so enough which might be why you slip sometimes. Tell you what, I'll make a deal with you, if I see you going over the edge I'll tell you, ok, even when we're 99years old."

"99? You think you'll hang around me that long?"

"Weeeeeell, got no other plans right now. The question is, will you want to be with me?"

He looked deep into her beautiful almond eyes and laughed.

"Just when I think you're smart, you go and say something stupid like that! Of course I want to be with you."

He paused.

"Baby, what were you trying to forget?"

Amy averted her gaze from Theo's warm smile to the chaos of the wind blowing the snow in little tornadoes outside. Her heart began beating faster and faster as fear gripped her once more.

Theo nuzzled closer to her as he whispered.

"It's ok. You can tell me. I'm not going anywhere either. Promise."

She was glad in this moment that the coffee shop was almost empty and as they sat at the bench looking out of the window she felt like there was a bubble of intimacy around them, nevertheless it was hard to find the courage.

"It happened two years ago. My, well that is my…"

The memories hurt and the words choked her throat.

"…well, you know my Dad walked out on us when I was a kid and then Mum met this guy, Frank. You know he was a real highflyer in the Loop, drove a Merc. took us to fancy restaurants, always had cash on the hip. I mean he was decent enough, and as I didn't have a Dad to compare him to he seemed ok. Bought me and my little Sis. anything we wanted…"

Theo's stomach was tightening. He was afraid of where this was going.

She cleared her throat as she continued.

"Well, I think Mum was kinda impressed with him and it made her feel good to have someone who took such good care of us but then…"

Amy fixed her gaze on a newsstand across the street so as to have focus and composure to finish.

"...Mum was out for a long weekend at a sales conference in Boston. He, he..." Her lips were trembling, and her mouth was dry.

"We had pizza on the second night... Joanne had a sleepover, so it was just me alone with him. He put something in my soda, I dunno what it was but it made me kinda dizzy.... I was conscious but you know couldn't really move much."

She glanced fleetingly at Theo whose despair for what was to come caused tears to fall down her cheeks as she focused back on that newsstand.

"...He, he touched me...I kinda remember telling him to stop but my voice was weird and then he... he raped me!"

The world seemed to stop spinning. Snow has a way of deadening sound but couldn't even compete with the deafening silence of those moments.

Theo pulled her closer and gently wiped away her tears with his hand. He didn't know what to say. What could he say. What could he do. All he knew was that he felt angry. Angry at himself for not allowing her to tell him before, angry at that, that man, angry at God and yet in all of that instant anger he also felt deep pain for her. The kind of kindred pain that signals a deep honest and true love for someone. He wanted to scream from the top of his lungs, just to show her his love, solidarity, and anger on her behalf.

He wanted her to know that he would protect and shield her from the world, so that she would never ever be hurt again. Then his thoughts were shattered.

"I'm so ashamed. What kind of whore am I!"

Theo stared at her in disbelief.

"Huh? You are not, not a whore! And you have nothing to be ashamed of."

"I'm sorry."

"What? What the... don't you ever, ever say that word ever again about this..."

"I'm dirty Theo. I'll understand if you don't want to be with me anymore. Actually I wouldn't blame you. It's ok, you can find a girl who doesn't have hang-ups like me."

"Baby. If you only knew how wrong that is, if you only knew..."

He stopped. This was a momentous moment.

"Knew what?"

Theo held her hands in his and looked her straight in the eye.

"I'm a mess. I'm broken and screwed up, well ah, huh guess you know that but what you don't know is, well the thing is... baby I'm in love with you!"

Cathartic, healing beautiful tears flowed down both faces as they melted into each other's arms before the chat continued.

"It took me a long time to tell Mum, but when I did she called the cops on him. I mean he skipped town before they got to him but maybe one day there'll be justice. And, and I started counselling couple of months back. I knew you were special and knew I had to confront and deal with all of it. I'm sorry I never told you any of it, but..."

Theo kissed her on the lips.

"Nah-uh, I told you not to use that 's' word. We're in this together. Broken together, but always together."

Part Fourteen

They talked for a while longer allowing healing to begin before Amy suddenly jumped up.

"Babe! It's game time soon. We need to get you to the field."

Theo pulled her back onto her stool and shook his head.

"Nah, this is more important."

"Hey, it's ok, we have all the time in the world to talk, besides I'm pretty tired now."

Theo's body language spoke volumes.

"Theo? What is it?"

"I think I'm done with football."

"What? Why? Thought you love the game!"

"Yeah, yeah I do but you know, Coach Murphy... I mean I he, it's just too stressful, and I need to start getting rid of those things I can't deal with."

Amy nodded.

"Yeah, I get that Babe, and I'll support you whatever you decide, but I know you'll hate yourself if you don't turn up tonight. You've never let them down before and I know you don't want to now. Listen, it's ok, you know, I mean it doesn't matter what happens, if you win or lose. I don't care, your Mum and Sis don't care. What matters to us is that you are happy, and I know you are happy on the field. We love you no matter what. You are priceless to us and so valuable to the team."

She paused.

"Babe, no pressure, honest. If you decide not to play then you have my full support, but hey you got that either way and whatever happens."

....

The stadium was packed to the rafters with cheering fans, and it felt like most of the town were out in support. The ground team had worked hard to clear the snow and as the hot dog vendors and beer merchants did a brisk trade, the school marching brass band attempted to keep the crowd in warm spirits despite the falling temperature.

The Eagles locker room was full. Full of expectation energy and nerves, full of anticipation egos and testosterone.

"100%. Nothing more nothing less!"

Coaches pre-game team talks were legendary for all the wrong reasons and his style of intimidation threats and fear introduced levels of tension beyond anything else. Now as he drew his speech to a close he roared at the top of his voice.

"No mercy. One unit. One victory."

"Coach! Yes Coach" The team boomed in military unison.

Theo instinctively murmured a silent prayer as he grabbed his helmet and joined the others marching down the corridor towards the floodlit field and the ever growing almost deafening roar of the crowd. There was no doubt about it as he emerged from the tunnel, he felt all at once utterly consumed by the moment, intimidated by the already outrageous expectations and yet also strangely high on being on the receiving end of such a force of will and support from the crowd. He felt like he was stepping in to save the day, maybe yes another version of the hulk would show itself today and he would transform into the hero everyone wanted. He couldn't help but be lifted up and swept along by the power of the support surrounding him and his team mates especially as the speakers blasted out lyrics that would puff up anyone's ego,

"...I'm the definition of tragedy turned triumph, it's David and Goliath; I made it to the eye of the storm..."

For these brief moments Theo felt strong and determined. He forgot his own struggles and trials and even managed to believe in himself. Of course he knew how frail and fragile and ultimately how vacuous these feelings were. He knew you could be riding high one moment, adored by a loving crowd chanting your name and then, one mistake, one loss later hated and vilified, rejected and condemned. It was a fickle way to spend your life, but he knew teammates who lived for this, for the feeling of being held aloft and would do anything in their power to stay in the favour of the fans. They had little else to lean on, to look to or to fill their lives. Despite his own struggles, his own lack of self-worth and the darkness that caused such despair, at least Theo didn't feel this way which was ironic considering how on a day-to-day basis he knew one of his weaknesses was to be liked by those around him and how he would sacrifice his own wellbeing to get that fix. To him however, it was his family and friends from where he drew strength and security, and they were all that truly mattered at the end of the day.

....

Nevertheless, Theo felt it, that unmistakable buzz, that flood of endorphins filling every fibre of his being.

It felt like a gladiatorial fight to the finish or was it more like the Christians being thrown to the lions? Either way the whole team was pumped, energised and the combined self-belief of the players along with the lift of the crowd and let's face it the fear of letting coach down all seemed to click as the whistle blew and the first quarter got under way.

The Washington Browns were a formidable opponent, as strong and determined as the Eagles and, it seemed to many, had picked their team based not only on skill but intimidation too. Each and every one looked like a giant of muscle and power, but the Eagles knew their weaknesses, had studied their plays long and hard and as the game began they quickly took the lead.

Theo was deep in the game to begin with, and his skill and ability meant he was the best kind of player you could hope for, quick to steal the ball, a great throwing arm and a generous ability to block and give his team mates the chance for glory.

In the vast crowd, Mom Faith and Amy cheered Theo and the Eagles, screamed injustice at just about every move of the Browns and did their best to take their minds of off the freezing night.

At the start of the second quarter, the Eagles had a comfortable lead and although Theo hadn't made any particular special plays, he knew he had assisted the team exactly as was expected of him and was happy with his performance as going into half time they walked off the field fired up by a 12-4 lead.

Of course Coach wasn't happy and picked apart every play like some kind of sports forensic investigator, telling each one how much more they could offer and that a win was only worth it if earned. His tactics were simple, wind them up enough to fire them up to see results out there, after all he had played in and coached enough games over the years to know nothing is certain until the final whistle.

And his rationale was about to become all too real as almost immediately in the third quarter the Eagles seemed to stumble, and the Browns quickly took advantage with two very fast and very easy touchdowns. None of the Eagles dared look over at Coach who was jumping up and down like a demented jack in the box, screaming every expletive known to man and some brand new.

Bodies crashed crunched and collided as the warriors on both sides saw the Eagles lead quickly diminish. Tackles became more violent and severe, and it seemed as if the groundskeeper would spend forever mopping up the blood and picking up teeth.

The end of the third saw the Browns close the gap to just two points and it was a hurting depleted and shattered Eagles team who huddled at the start of the fourth.

Sweat and blood covered faces and bodies, but the determination of the team seemed enough to ignore the pain.

They clasped hands together.

"No mercy. One unit. One victory."

Determination, survival instinct, call it what you will but in what would go down as one of the most exciting nail-biting clashes in the history of these two teams, the Eagles powered on in plays and set pieces that dazzled and impressed but still, try as they might, they couldn't break the lead. Then with just 58 seconds left on the clock, the opportunity came to employ one of Coaches own set pieces that could steal the lead and bring victory in those dying seconds.

They had practiced it over and over. Coach had insisted on pushing this play more than any other, one that would isolate Theo deep in centre field while his team mates effectively deceived the Browns into believing they were attacking elsewhere. It was brave, foolish and brilliant to 'run the valley' but now was the time.

Kidd and Limula blocked while 'killer' broke loose. Theo was flanked by Shay and Elliot before he slipped out and dashed down the field, turning to see 'killer' smash his way through two quarterbacks and into the ten-yard zone as Gibson threw the ball into Theo's possession. He ran with the ball, swerved and avoided one, two, three players spotting the mark to throw the ball into 'killers' hands for a sure-fire touchdown and certain victory. It had been labelled 'run the valley' for good reason as Browns players quickly aware of the deceit were now bearing down on him.

Theo had gone over this play a million times in his head and the irony of comparison to how this play simulated his life wasn't lost on him. He often felt isolated in life and constantly running, often finding himself in his own private dark valley where he felt he could never escape. The giants of the Browns closing in on him felt all the world like his own thoughts and emotions trying with all their might to tackle him to the ground. Then there was the expectation, rational or not, real or not of how he thought all eyes were on him just waiting to screw up, surely represented by Coach his teammates and the crowd.

Unlike life, the move was well rehearsed, well-practiced and Theo had been chosen for the strength of his arm to make what for him was an easy throw, but in that split second his focus wobbled and as the clock counted down, 7,6,5,4... he hesitated to grip the ball better and then he leant his body back ready to launch the most important pass of his career.

3,2,1.

The full-time whistle blew! The crowd erupted. The local news network reporter was going crazy!

Theo lay there, exhausted and with excruciating pain coursing through his knee. He felt nauseous and dizzy but as much as he felt like he was in a dream, he was also all too aware of the moment and instead of a dream, it was a nightmare.

The two Brown players who had tackled him to the ground were doing their victory dance above him and then to add insult to injury threw the retrieved ball at his chest.

"Why?" He thought to himself, "Why did I hesitate? The grip was good enough!"

Moments can sometimes feel like hours or even days and a million thoughts can travel around your brain in those times. Theo wondered if this was actually one of those self-destruct moments. Did he think he didn't deserve to be victorious with the team. Maybe he just wanted Coach and the team to hate him as much as he did himself sometimes. One other little voice bugged him more than any other as the stretcher team lead him off and as his teammates shook their heads at him. One little voice of reason... or rationality. Maybe it wasn't deliberate. Maybe you did your best. Maybe stuff just happens. Maybe it's ok. After all, it's not life and death.

A difficult voice to listen to as Coaches face came into view.

....

Epilogue: Part One

The fireworks were spectacular and as well as lighting up the sky, shook the snow loose on the ground.

Watching them, Theo remembered recent weeks.

....

The weeks since that fateful game had been the classic cliché of a rollercoaster for Theo, as he continued to deal with his depression and also the added fallout from the defeat where it felt everyone in Lincoln Grove was staring and pointing at him as if had singlehandedly and deliberately lost the game. Truth be told he still struggled with that last point himself and at times felt even less like he knew who he truly was.

From rather negative headlines in the local newspaper to a distinct rejection by his peers who would very deliberately ignore him as they passed by in school and not to mention the numerous comments on social media it was amazing that he even got out of bed on some days. However, yesterday's news is old news before the tweet is even sent and it actually didn't take long before attention was focused on someone else, some other poor unsuspecting innocent victim.

Of course Theo's family, Amy and friends stuck by him and were a constant source of encouragement but following a visit to the doctor and concerns about the injury to his knee, coupled with what he had already been thinking, Theo decided to 'retire' from the game.

It had been a hard decision, and yet one that he had a strange peace about and even Coach Murphy seemed unusually calm about it. Theo had expected a real taking down but instead Coach was silent, the kind of stony silence that says a lot while saying nothing at all and can be interpreted a hundred ways. Coach cleared his throat as Theo turned to walk out of his office.

"Ahem, Y'know I can't pretend you didn't let everyone down and I'm not sure this so-called knee 'injury' of yours is excuse enough to give up! But, ahem, well suffice to say you weren't the worst player I've ever had the misfortune to come across."

He stood up and thrust a piece of paper into Theo's hand.

"There's a raw talent in you son. Maybe you shouldn't walk away from the game altogether! Now get outta my sight!"

As he walked out of the school Theo read the leaflet looking for coaches to train pee wee football. His heart skipped a beat. "Yes" He blurted out not caring who might hear him, "Yes, that's it!"

He had followed through immediately and within two weeks had begun coaching the game he loved to a team of young hopefuls where he was determined to teach in a way that would bring out the best in them in a strong but confidence building way.

....

As the fireworks continued to thunder and explode lighting up the sky on this New Year's Eve, Theo felt Amy cuddle close as Mom smiled reassuringly at him.

"It's freezing." Amy whispered as Theo drew her closer.

"I got you babe."

....

They had talked often and deep over these last few weeks and their relationship had broadened and strengthened, cemented on Christmas Day when Amy spent the day at Theo's. That evening after Mom and Faith had gone to bed, Theo and Amy curled up on the sofa and as they listened to some music by candlelight, Theo produced a small square gift-wrapped box.

Amy's heart felt like it would explode through her chest but before she could open it, Theo spoke.

"Babe, I don't know what I've done to deserve you. I can't for the life of me figure out why you wanna stick around with a bum like me, but I'm glad you do. Listen, I'm far from perfect, y'know, I'm screwed up, messed up and still got this black dog chasing me, but I'm trying. Trying to overcome, trying to be more, and you make me wanna be better. I can't imagine life without you. You know I'm broken.."

She put her finger on his lips.

"Broken together, always together! Remember!"

Tears filled her eyes as she unwrapped the gift and opened the box to reveal a beautiful promise ring.

"Broken together" Theo repeated.

....

Depression, doubts and insecurities continued to chase Theo. Some days turned to weeks where things didn't feel so bad, but the very nature of things is that sometimes for no logical explanation you're tripped up.

Charlotte continued to help him use the 'tools' to tackle those times and to keep vigilant even on his better days. There were times he felt guilty his counselling seemed to be going on with no sight of an end but her reassurance that she was there for him for however long he needed it was key to his survival at times. That little oasis of safe space each week would often prove to be lifesaving.

....

As the fireworks came to an end Mom picked up a very tired Faith in her arms, leant over and kissed both Theo and Amy.

"Time to get this little one home and to bed." She smiled. "Happy New Year you two. I love you!"

"Love you!" They echoed together.

Theo and Amy walked home arm in arm. They remained silent for a while, just happy to be in that moment. The new year could and would undoubtedly do it's terrible and wonderful dance around them. Good and bad times were bound to come their way but right here, right now they could nothing about any of that. All they could do, all they wanted to do was to live and enjoy this moment.

Insecurities, guilt, depression, hurt, failure, regret. These things were not far from the front of their minds, but each day was a new start and actually they didn't need a new year to reset and start over as they could do that any day they wanted. True, sometimes those lying voices of accusation and deceit got the better of them, but at the end of the day they were as good as anyone else. Who was to say or dictate what they were or what they could become. Of course it wasn't that easy, but they would keep on keeping on.

With all this in mind, Theo broke the silence.

He was still battling this thing called life and still trying to work out his place and reason to justify why he awoke each morning.

"I dunno. I just don't know what my purpose is. I mean, I know I'm loved by you, Moms Faith and others and I love you all, but I'm not sure I've ever made a real-life changing impact."

Amy nodded.

"I know. I feel the same. Maybe we'll never know."

Theo kissed her.

"Just hope I can make a difference one day."

Epilogue: Part Two

She took a bite out of her burger and closed her eyes. It may have only been the plainest cheapest one on the menu, but it felt like a banquet after all this time. Then she wrapped her bony hands around the steaming hot coffee and as she began to feel like her body was thawing out, gazed out onto the city battling another blizzard. Her thoughts went back to earlier that morning and how she had thought as though the bitter cold might actually get the better of her this time and how as she had shivered and felt fear and regret consuming her just as those two sweet young kids had stopped to chat with her.

They made a cute couple, she thought to herself but there was something genuine and honest about them. A life on the streets taught you all sorts of lessons such as how to survive and deal with the abuse often thrown your way. Sadly it also taught you, if you let it, to be cynical, selfish and mistrusting of human motives but she had determined during the almost three years on the streets that she had lost too much already to abandon her sense of dignity and belief in the common good. It wasn't easy when she was often verbally abused and had been beaten on numerous occasions but just when she was beginning to lose hope and even began to contemplate ending it all, along came these two.

The girl had looked a little nervous and actually even the boy seemed rather apprehensive, but it was he who had taken the lead, first of all handing her a few bucks from his pocket but then he had turned back and smiled at her.

"I'm Theo and this is Amy!"

Through chapped lips and a dry throat she gazed up at him.

"Maria!"

"Hey Maria! Nice to meet you. Is there some place we can take you, a shelter maybe?"

Maria shook her head. Most of the shelters were full at this time of the year but actually her last experience had left her swearing she would never go back. She shivered again and Theo glanced at Amy before removing his scarf and giving it to her.

"Bet your family must be missing you, Maria. Do you have kids?"

She nodded.

"Yeah, bet they miss you. You know, I lost my Pops last year. I would give anything to just be able to speak to him again. I don't care what might have happened, but there's nothing else that matters."

Maria stared at Theo and Amy with almost lifeless eyes. Pain and regret filled her heart as she thought about the life she once had and more importantly the family she had left behind. Life has a funny way of dealing your hand she thought to herself. One minute you're riding high, a great job, money flowing in your account, a loving husband and two beautiful daughters then almost in a heartbeat everything changes.

She had been stupid to have the affair in the first place but although no excuse, he had charmed her and had ulterior motives so within six months of secret rendezvous and all the lies she told her family, he had hacked her account, taken every last cent and disappeared. Then her company was wrongly accused of illegal trading and the very sigma of this caused clients to drop their contracts like rocks in the ocean. In no time at all she was bankrupt, the house was repossessed and then with no healthcare plan in place the worst scenario hit when her husband was diagnosed with a terminal illness and they couldn't afford the proper palliative care.

The truth of the affair came crashing out, her husband passed, and she had the biggest falling out with her daughters. Guilt and shame took over and she said many hurtful things to cover her own feelings of failure before she had stormed out that fateful day.

She had no clue as to where she was going or what she was going to do and aside from the clothes she was standing up in, only had a few dollars to her name. She tried to make it, took a little job working in a coffee shop but was fired for no reason after just three weeks and was then thrown out of her one room apartment when she couldn't pay rent and refused to make it up with the advances of the sleazy landlord.

That was the first night she slept on the streets. She had vowed it would be the only one but that was three years ago. She believed that in her heart she was a good person, but one who had made mistakes, but the spiral downwards had been so fast, and it felt with each passing day harder to break free. It was her mistakes that had given her the determination to regain some kind of decency and optimism but again she thought back to those dark thoughts and then remembered the young man's smile. She was desperate to go home.

Theo spoke softly to Maria as Amy hooked her arm in his.

"They need you, and what do you have to lose!"

She was desperate to see her daughters but so full of fear. Fear of how they must hate her. Fear of unforgiveness and fear of rejection and yet she had seen such kindness in Theo and Amy that gave her courage to take one final chance.

She finished her coffee and as the hot beverage warmed her tummy wracked with nerves walked outside to a payphone, picked up the receiver and dialled her daughter's number.

"Hello…"

"He had cried before but never like this. This was pure undiluted sobbing. Weeping as if from his very soul, a purging of something very deep inside as if there was a massive ache that was consuming his whole being desperate to escape via this river of tears. And yet within this attempt at freedom, to be released from such excruciating pain, Theo strangely felt nothing. It was like he was being held captive by some inner demon intent on his demise.
Before, when the tears had flowed, it had been therapeutic, cathartic and although leaving him utterly drained would somehow serve a purpose, but this, this was having no such apparent end game."

....

According to a study by the World Health Organisation (WHO), globally, more than 264 million people of all ages suffer from depression.

Sadly as much as we may like to pat ourselves on the back, the fact of the matter is many who struggle with depression still hide it from family friends and work colleagues. There is a silent shame and a false stigma to this issue that means the likelihood is the real figure given by WHO is much higher.

"We all get down sometimes. Pull yourself together. Have a positive mindset. Be grateful for what you have. You've got it so much better than others"...

Anyone who battles depression or acute anxiety knows the truth. If it was as easy as just putting on a smile and skipping off into the sunset then we would be there already, and for goodness sake if you only knew how much I give thanks for all I have. Although there are many variations such as Panic Disorder, Stress, Social Anxiety etc., all with their own complex symptoms and individual effects, the most common types of depression are summed up either "reactive" or "organic". The first is self-explanatory, the kind that engulfs you after a major trauma. Respond quick enough with support and help and this may only ever be a season, whilst the second is defined by the root cause not being addressed and allowed to take a much deeper hold or a chemical imbalance.

Depression is as unstable and as unpredictable as a dormant volcano. It strikes with no rhyme or reason and like the lava that destroys everything in its path, depression also consumes.

The National Institute of Mental Health (NIMH) estimates that 1 in 5 people will struggle with mental illness of one form or another, meaning that unless you live alone in a cabin on a mountaintop you will be into contact with someone who is affected.

You are not alone. Winston Churchill, Bruce Springsteen, Anne Hathaway, JK Rowling, Dwayne Johnson are just a few names on a very long list of prominent public figures who have admitted to their personal battles. The point being, depression does not discriminate and nobody, but nobody is immune.

It's a scary thing to think you may have this "black dog" (as Churchill described it) always at your heel. As alluded to earlier, this world is still full of ignorant uneducated people who won't understand but thankfully there are many more who do.

Depression is never anyone's fault. You don't wake up one morning and say, "today I think I'll be depressed" but when it does bite you it's devastating.

Eleonor Roosevelt famously said, "Nobody can make you feel inferior without your consent." This is so powerful and so true.

It is said that authors often reveal themselves between the lines they write. No such hidden characterisation in Run the Valley, for my heart is very much worn on the page here as my own struggle with depression takes centre stage.

TJ's fight, his feelings his thoughts are I guess, autobiographical shining a little pinprick of light into what can be a very dark environment as his struggles mirror my own experiences. Although the setting and backdrop do not reflect my own privileged lifestyle, (artistic licence takes a front row seat), the narrative certainly does.

This book touches on the story of a central character who has had sadness and grief in his young life, but actually lives in a nice neighbourhood, has a loving family, loyal friends and attends a good school. He's not an academic over achiever, but neither is he dim and although an intricate part of the football team, he is never going to set

the sporting world on fire. Theo is a classic everyday "hero", someone who is just a "normal" (whatever that word really means) likeable guy, the sort of person who just gets on with life, who is never really noticed. In other words, Theo is what most of us are, an "average joe".
Theo is not suicidal. He doesn't struggle with bipolar disorder or harbour thoughts of self-harm. His struggles with his mental health are not extreme in any sense but rather like his own personality, his depression could also be characterised as "average". Herein lays the danger, to dismiss his struggles because they are not dramatic or even life threatening when in actual fact it can be a suffocating beast, debilitating monster, and crippling disability.

Sometimes life just weighs us down and there may not be any particular life altering cataclysmic event that sends us down that rabbit hole, but the struggle pain and despair is still suffocating, and all too real.
This book does not offer any kind of fix or solution because everyone and anyone who has struggled with mental health issues knows that their own battle is unique and therefore the road to recovery and freedom has to be a personal journey. Of course there are things that can be done, basic steps to move us forward and while some may indeed find a full and lasting recovery, for others it's a day at a time working out how best to manage what may be a long-term challenge.

We are told that this is a more enlightened world when it comes to mental health, but my own experiences have still found ignorant thinking and attitudes. Mental health is thankfully talked about in today's world in a way it never has been before and yet it can still be a taboo subject and can even elicit shame on the part of those who often struggle in silence. It is not always as easy as being "grateful" for what you have or just being "positive", but the world at large just does not get that.

Sadly, depression and mental health issues are on the increase. Maybe it's just that we are more comfortable talking about it, maybe the stresses of life are notching up a gear, but it is an epidemic that we must address. It is estimated that 10% of the world's population will personally face mental health issues of one kind or another, and 1 in 6 people report experiencing a mental health problem in any given week. Remember though, these figures are based on those who are prepared to admit it, so in actuality the number is far greater. And it's not always obvious. With those stats in mind, walk into a room with half a dozen people and the chances are at least one of them will be struggling with their mental health, but you may not realise. Why? Because they are probably the ones working hardest to tell a joke or deflect questions about themselves. Anything rather than expose their "shameful" darkness and then risk the reaction and fallout. I once sat my friends down to try and explain I was struggling with depression and one reaction was shocking to say the least, suggesting they were worried they may "catch" it from me.

Run the Valley is meant to highlight just a little of what it feels like to live in the skin of someone struggling with depression, but it is by no means pessimistic and instead encourages us to remember that despite the challenges and hardships we may face personally, we all matter and each and everyone has a place and purpose in this world. The story also dips it's toes into the troubled waters of the fallout from other pressures and stresses in this world as a reminder that no matter who we are, how we present ourselves we are all in this life together.

Every day you get up is a win. Every time you breathe is a reminder you are alive for a reason. Maybe, just maybe the courage it takes to get up, to breathe, actually shows more strength than those who pretend to have it all together. I'm not suggesting everyone else is harbouring secret depression nor that facing your problems makes you any more special, but I genuinely believe there is an immense bravery in admitting who you truly are, and in truth although you may feel lonely at times, you are not alone.

Sometimes the only focus is "when will this ever end" or "why can't I be free" but for many it's about managing the struggle, recognising that it's ok to not be ok and addressing potential triggers.
There is plenty of help, so don't be afraid to go out there and find it. Even though it's easy at times to feel otherwise, **depression does not define you. You are and will always be you.**

Printed in Great Britain
by Amazon

64814749R00052